DRAGON CHILD

The Sapphire Quest

GILL VICKERY

Illustrated by
MIKE LOVE

A & C BLACK
AN IMPRINT OF BLOOMSBURY
LONDON   NEW DELHI   NEW YORK   SYDNEY

■ Major Towns
● Villages
‡ Ports
⊛ Dragon Keeps
★ Dragon Haven

Volcanic
Keeps

West Eldkeiler
Mts

Stoplar

Western Sea

Hamar

Iserborg

Sanderhof

Northern Sea

Fellhof

West Eldkeiler Mts

Drakelow Mts

Eastern Sea

Kulafoss

Drangur

Holmurholt

Askarlend

Roornhof

Southern Sea

The Story So Far...

The High Witches of Tulay stole the DragonQueen's jewels of power and drove the dragons away. In revenge, one of the dragons kidnapped the youngest witch's child, Tia. Raised by the mighty creatures, Tia is now on a quest to retrieve the jewels, helped by her DragonBrother, Finn, who can blend invisibly into any background, and a jackdaw called Loki.

Tia has already stolen back three jewels: the emerald, which grants the power to talk to animals, the opal, which lets its owner change shape, and the topaz, which controls the weather.

Now Tia, disguised as a Trader called Nadya, has arrived at Stoplar. Stoplar is ruled by Skadi, who has the sapphire that enables the bearer to travel instantly from one place to another. But the three remaining High Witches have now learned of the thefts and Tia is in greater danger than ever before.

DRAGON CHILD

To Chris and Jennie -
DragonFather and DragonChild

First published 2013 by A & C Black,
an imprint of Bloomsbury Publishing Plc
50 Bedford Square
London WC1B 3DP

www.bloomsbury.com

ISBN 978-1-4081-8828-6

A CIP catalogue for this book is available from the British Library.

Printed and Bound by CPI Group (UK) Ltd, Croydon CR0 4YY

1 3 5 7 9 10 8 6 4 2

Chapter One

The Avenue of Beasts

Tia and her DragonBrother sat on a sloping hill of plumed cottongrass and scanned the skies. Finn's sharp dragon eyes were the first to spot a black dot high above the plain stretching away in front of them.

'There he is!'

Tia shaded her eyes with her hand and made out a jackdaw flying swiftly in their direction. He landed with a bounce on the grass.

'Well?' Tia demanded.

'Don't be so impatient,' the bird said and started to preen his feathers.

'What did he say?' the little copper-coloured dragon asked.

'He told me not to be impatient.'

Finn laughed and puffed out a smoke ring at Loki.

The bird shook his wings. 'That's better.' He cocked his head at Tia. 'I suppose you want a report?'

'Yes, please, Loki.'

The jackdaw flew onto Finn's shoulder so that he was eye to eye with Tia and said, 'To the west of Iserborg town there are a few big hills. They look as if they're covered in snow and ice but it's dust from the white stone that people quarry there.'

'That must be marble – you remember Luona's palace was covered with it?'

'Skadi's castle is grey stone but there are marble statues all over it.' Loki shook his wings. 'They're of horrible, ugly monsters. The castle's in the middle of the town and it's got a moat. There's a bridge at the front and a watergate at the back. The town's surrounded by a wall with two gates. Big stone avenues lead up to them, only...'

'Yes?' Tia prompted.

'There are more of those marble statues – huge ones – standing on each side of the avenues. I didn't like them.'

'Why not?'

But Loki wouldn't explain any further, except to say they looked bad and made him feel strange.

Tia told her DragonBrother what the jackdaw had said.

Finn's smoke rings came faster. 'I don't like the sound of those statues.'

'Neither do I,' Tia said, 'but I have to steal that sapphire from Skadi and I'd better get going.' She picked up her backpack. 'It's late and I want to get there before the town gates are closed at nightfall.'

Finn nudged Tia with his muzzle. 'I can disguise myself and take you part of the way.' He looked across the plain. 'I wonder where the spell boundary starts.'

Tia's witch powers meant she could see the spells that kept dragons away from the lands of the six towns. This one sparkled like frosted spider silk right around the plain. But she couldn't say so. She had to keep her powers secret from Finn because she didn't want him to know she was a 'witch-brat'. That was what the dragonets at Drakelow had called her.

'I think you ought to disguise yourself right away, just in case the spell's close,' she said.

Finn's skin rippled and turned to the colour of the cotton grass he was lying on. He picked Tia up and sprang into the air, changing into the colour of the evening sky as he flew.

They landed a safe distance away from Iserborg town, which was dominated by Skadi's squat, looming castle. Tia threw her arms around Finn's muzzle and told him to stay safe.

'I will,' he promised. 'And 'I'll be waiting for you when you get back.'

'I'll bring the sapphire with me.'

'You won't be tempted to use it?'

She shook her head vigorously. 'No!' She'd learned that the jewels were much too powerful for her to control safely, except for the emerald which she kept on a chain tucked safely away under her shirt. Finn kept the opal and topaz for her. She wouldn't risk using the sapphire, no matter how tempted she might be.

She gave Finn one last hug before he flew away then set off towards the town. Loki flew on ahead. The sun was beginning to set and he wanted to roost before darkness fell.

When Tia reached the avenue leading to the town gates, a chill ran through her. The marble beasts on either side were much, much bigger than she had imagined – three times the size of a large horse – and even more terrifying.

The first two creatures were a wolf, on her left, and a serpent, on her right. The wolf was carved in a crouching position as if it were ready to spring, its lips drawn back to show huge fangs. The serpent reared up on a column of coils, its tongue darting out like a spear. They looked horribly real, especially

in the failing light, and Tia felt her insides churn as she walked closer.

She stepped onto the avenue meaning to keep her eyes on the ground, but a loud grinding noise startled her and she looked up. The statues' heads had swivelled towards her. Their mouths gaped wider and their eyes lit up with a deep red glow.

Tia's heart pounded. Would they leap on her as she passed them? Holding her breath, she walked steadily forward. The ghastly grating noise started up again as the beasts' heads twisted and their red eyes followed her progress down the avenue.

A few strides more and she came to the next two beasts, a bear and a leopard. Their snarling heads twisted round too and their red eyes fixed on her. Skadi must have put a spell on the statues to make them move whenever anyone approached. It was strong magic. No wonder Loki had felt uneasy.

Tia hurried on. She passed animals she recognised, a pine marten and a lynx, and animals she didn't – a great cat with a collar of shaggy fur and a plumed tail, an armoured bull-like creature with a vicious horn on its nose. They were all the same size and all had moving heads and glowing eyes that followed her every step. By the time she reached the gates she was running. She shot into the town and across a square into a higgledy-piggledy collection of thatched houses.

Panting hard, she skidded to a stop halfway down a shadowy side street. She made sure she had a good view of the gates and then slumped underneath a window, recovering her breath.

In the square, people stood in anxious knots, talking in low, agitated voices. Even the guards at the entrance were deep in a tense conversation. Tia realised that was why they hadn't noticed her. She'd been lucky they had other things on their mind than a running child.

A light came on in the window above Tia's head and she heard talking.

'She wants five men for the quarries and seven women and children for servants,' a man's voice said.

'But she took nine folk last month!' a woman replied.

'There are accidents in the quarries and you know what happens when she tires of servants.'

The woman gave a cry of fright. 'But she won't take anyone now – you know she doesn't like to use the bracelet at night. Close the shutters and bolt the doors to be on the safe side.'

Tia heard the shutters above her being pulled to.

As the man locked them down he muttered, 'Not that bolts and bars can keep *her* out.'

All over the town, lights were being lit and shutters closed. The guards hauled the great wooden gates shut and barred them with stout beams. As darkness fell, two new guards with flaming torches marched up and the others strode off towards the castle. The night guards each went to a hut, one on either side of the gate, fixed their torches over the top and sat inside. The whole town fell quiet and the night closed in at last.

Chapter Two

The secret cellar

Tia leaned back against the wall and thought about the conversation she'd overheard. What did the woman mean by saying High Witch Skadi 'took' people?

Malindra had used animals to keep her citizens under control, Yordis had turned herself into a bear and threatened to eat people, and Luona froze anyone who crossed her. But what could Skadi do with the sapphire that frightened the people of Iserborg so much?

A cold wind scurried across the square. Tia shivered. Summer was close but the nights were still cold and she needed to find shelter. She wished Loki didn't roost at night; he'd be useful in finding her a place to go. A large piece of paper blew against her leg. As she pulled it off she saw it was a notice of some sort, with a picture of a face. It was too dark to see clearly but something about the face made Tia feel uneasy. She decided to look at it properly.

She went further down the street, hid in a doorway, and snapped a tiny light on the end of her finger. She gasped at what she saw. The picture was of her own face.

Hurriedly she read the notice:

HAVE YOU SEEN THIS CHILD?

She is a thief, known by the name of Nadya. Bring her to the Lady Skadi and receive a reward of 500 silver marks.

Tia had never heard of so much money. No-one would help her if that was the reward Skadi offered for her capture. She'd have to hide quickly – but where?

A scraping noise from the end of the street made Tia put out the flame and spin round. To her astonishment a trapdoor rose up and three children, one of them very small, climbed out into the street. They closed the trapdoor and scurried off.

Tia wondered who on earth they could be. She hurried to the end of the road and saw an alley running behind the houses. Feeling sure that the children had gone that way and wouldn't see her, Tia hauled on an iron ring set into the trapdoor. It lifted to reveal a gaping black hole. *Let's see what's down there,* she thought. *It might be a useful place for me to hide.*

She clicked another small flame onto her fingertip and leaned into the hole. Inside it looked like a cellar; maybe an old store for fire-rock. There were stools and a table and shelves. As she wriggled forward to take a better look, something shoved her in the back and she tumbled into the blackness. She banged her head as she landed, and fell into an even deeper darkness.

'Is she dead?' a small voice asked.

'No,' another voice answered. 'She knocked herself out. Serve her right for breaking into our cellar. It's a good job we heard the trapdoor creak and came back to see what was happening.'

Tia's head ached, but she was glad to know she was alive. She opened her eyes. Sitting in front of her, their backs against the wall, was a girl of about her own age and a very small boy. Light came from an oil lamp standing nearby.

'You're awake then,' the girl said.

Tia struggled up and discovered that her wrists and ankles were tied. 'I'm not dangerous,' she said. 'I was just looking in your cellar because I need a place to hide.'

'That's because you're a thief, running away from Skadi. We saw the poster. There's a big reward offered for you.'

Even though Tia's head was hurting, she thought quickly. The children wouldn't be able to turn her in to the High Witch without being caught themselves. 'You're hiding as well, aren't you?' she asked.

The girl glared.

'Does Skadi want you?' Tia went on, trying to sound friendly.

The girl nodded slowly. 'She wanted our family,'

she said, hugging the little boy, 'to punish our father for daring to ask her not to take people. Father was her steward and she made him go and haul marble in the quarry. He was killed. She made Mother her maid and my older brother, Ingvar, and me chimney sweepers.' She hugged the small boy tighter. 'And she said she'd take Sindri to be her son.'

Tia thought about her DragonMother, Freya, who'd brought her up as her own DragonChild. She was kind and Tia loved her. Skadi wasn't like that. 'What happened to your mother?' she asked.

'The High Witch took her. She tried to run away with me and my brothers but Skadi appeared. Mother struggled with her and Skadi had to let go of us. Mother shouted, "Run!" So we did. I looked back and saw Skadi take her. We're going to wait until Mother finds us again one day.'

Tia remembered her father promising to find her when the great dragon Andgrim snatched her away. *I'll find you, Tia! I'll find you and bring you back!* he'd called. She was still waiting.

'I was stolen too,' Tia said.

The girl's eyes widened. 'Who took you?'

Tia couldn't tell the truth, that Andgrim had kidnapped her because her mother was one of the High Witches who'd stolen the dragons' jewels of power. 'Malindra,' she said, 'the High Witch of Drangur. I'm good with animals and she wanted me to help look after her menagerie. When her emerald of power was stolen and the people caught her, I ran away. My parents are Traders and they'd moved on. I've been going to all the towns trying to find them.'

Noises from overhead put an end to the conversation. The trapdoor opened and a boy swung down, locking it behind him.

'Ingvar!' The little boy leapt up and hurled himself at his brother. 'Have you brought us lots to eat?'

Ingvar put a sack onto the table. 'Plenty of food!' he said. 'But I couldn't finish all the tasks by myself. It's a shame you had to stay behind after I pushed her in here.' He jerked his thumb in Tia's direction. 'Now we need to decide what to do about her.'

He and the girl went into a corner and talked in low, urgent voices while Sindri rummaged in the sack. Tia wondered where the food had come from and what Ingvar had meant by 'finishing tasks'.

Ingvar and his sister nodded in agreement and came back towards her.

'Bryndis says she trusts you – that's good enough for me,' the boy said. He untied her bonds. 'You can hide here while you look for your parents.'

'Thank you.' Tia rubbed her tingling wrists and ankles. 'Can I do anything in return?'

'Maybe tomorrow night. Now we eat and then we sleep while it's day.'

The food Ingvar had brought was very good. There were steaming pies wrapped in cloth to keep them warm, crusty bread, cheese and fruit.

When they'd finished and cleared away Bryndis showed Tia to a heap of blankets by the wall. Her bag was on the top. 'You can sleep here.'

Tia thanked her and lay down. She wished she was snuggled up to Finn with the stars overhead and Loki nearby, sleeping with his head under his wing. But she was warm and safe here. Now she'd be able to look for the sapphire and plan how to steal it from Skadi. *It's strange, though,* she thought as she drifted off to sleep, *they live in a cellar but their food is good and these blankets are thick and warm – and clean.* Before she could puzzle about it any more she was fast asleep.

Chapter Three

The Elves of Iserborg Castle

'Wake up!' Tia opened her eyes to find Bryndis shaking her. 'We need to get going. Ingvar wasn't able to finish the tasks by himself yesterday and we'll have to start as soon as possible tonight to make up for it.'

Tia scrambled to her feet, wondering what the mysterious tasks were.

Ingvar went first, unlocking the trapdoor and peering out cautiously before pulling himself up into the street. Tia, Sindri and Bryndis followed. They ran silently down the shadowy alley and round the streets until they reached the back of the castle. It was encircled by a moat with water plants, lush shrubbery and trees growing around it.

They stopped at the water's edge.

'How are we going to get in?' Tia whispered. 'We can't swim the moat, we'll get soaked.'

Bryndis rolled her eyes at her elder brother as if to say, *What a weakling!* Ingvar laughed and reached into some shrubbery. He untied the end of a hidden rope knotted to a branch, and tugged. A small boat floated out from among the reeds. Tia and Sindri climbed into the back while Ingvar and Bryndis took the oars. They rowed across the moat, leaving silver ripples in their wake.

As they drew nearer, the bright moonlight lit up swarms of grotesque marble creatures covering the castle. They peered from window frames and round corners, from roofs and sheer walls that they clung to with long claws. Their hideous faces grinned down. Tia shivered and looked away.

The boat bumped against a narrow gateway barred by a locked iron gate. Bryndis expertly kept the little boat steady while Ingvar stood and picked the lock. The gate swung open without a sound. *They must keep the hinges well oiled,* Tia thought approvingly.

With the boat moored tightly to the watergate they ran up a flight of stone steps and into the castle. The four of them moved swiftly through shady corridors lit by flickering torches. Tia memorised landmarks

as they rushed past tapestries and fantastic statues, all as ugly as the sneering gargoyles on the outside of the castle.

Abruptly they stopped. Ingvar cautiously opened a huge door and stuck his head round it. He looked out again and waved cheerfully to show it was safe to enter.

Inside was an enormous kitchen illuminated by wavering tapers and a glow of fire-rock from two great hearths. Shadows danced on a vaulted ceiling supported by smoke-blackened beams. Cupboards lined the walls and a long table with benches on either side ran down the length of the room. There was a heap of clothing at one end and foodstuffs laid out on a white cloth in the middle.

Bryndis tugged Tia's sleeve. 'Come on.' She led the way to one of the hearths. 'We need to get the fire going.'

Tia pumped a pair of bellows and Bryndis heaped fresh fire-rock on the embers. When the flames were burning well she put a large pot of water on a rack over the top.

'Now what do we do?' Tia asked.

Bryndis grinned. 'We do our tasks,' she said.

The night passed in a whirl of work. The four children washed pans and pots, scoured the flagstone floor, mended clothes, washed laundry and scrubbed shoes. Tia was weary when they'd finished, and hungry.

Ingvar put the last shoe neatly by the hearth and said, 'Done! Now let's wash and eat.'

Bryndis warmed up slices of cold pie in the stone ovens in the hearth and pushed fish wrapped in wet leaves among the ashes of the fire while Ingvar cut up bread and cheese. Sindri and Tia laid plates, knives and goblets on the cloth and poured water from a jug. Then they sat at the table and dined in style.

When Tia felt she couldn't eat another crumb, she said, 'I don't understand – who leaves you this work? Why do they feed you and why do they serve you food on such fine plates?'

The children laughed. 'It's the castle servants – they think we're night elves who do their work in exchange for food and clothes,' Bryndis told her.

'Don't they ever try and catch you?' Tia asked.

Bryndis shook her head. 'They know the elves will leave if anyone tries to trap them.'

Tia had heard stories about elves from the Traders. If you annoyed them they made mischief, so people were always respectful, just in case.

'And we make sure to leave well before dawn,' Ingvar said, getting to his feet. 'That way we're never seen.'

Tia was disappointed. She'd hoped to have time to explore the castle and find out where Skadi was and, more importantly where she kept her sapphire. *I can do that another time*, she thought as she followed Bryndis and Ingvar back to the watergate.

In the boat Sindri leaned against her and fell asleep. She woke him when they reached the other

side of the moat and he held her hand all the way
back to the cellar.

Tia worked well with Bryndis, Ingvar and Sindri
and soon fitted in with them. She began to enjoy
living with the little family but it made her miss her
DragonBrother terribly. She fretted about Finn. She
knew he would be worried about her but, as she
never saw Loki by night and the trapdoor was always
securely locked by day, she couldn't ask the jackdaw
to take a message to the little dragon.

She concentrated on learning about Iserborg
castle – and High Witch Skadi. On nights when
there weren't too many tasks the children went
exploring, and Tia soon got to know the castle layout
well. Skadi's rooms were in a tower at the very top
of the castle. 'We don't go there,' Bryndis said one
night as they sat in front of the kitchen fire. 'It's too
dangerous.'

'There's guards,' Sindri said, his eyes wide, 'in
the sapphire room where she leaves the bracelet at
night.'

'Why does she do that?' Tia asked the two older children who were frowning at Sindri.

'Because if she had a bad dream the sapphire would take her to the place of her nightmares,' Bryndis said.

Sindri opened his mouth to speak but Ingvar held up his hand. 'Hush!' he ordered. Tia knew they weren't going to tell her any more about Skadi or the sapphire. She'd just have to find out for herself.

Chapter Four

The Stone Guards

Tia's chance came one night as they sat in front of the fire playing a game of counters. Sindri had won and was very pleased with himself.

Tia jumped up. 'I'm tired of sitting – let's go and explore.'

Sindri's face fell. 'One more game, please,' he pleaded.

'All right,' Ingvar agreed. 'Just one.'

'I don't mind exploring on my own,' Tia said, trying not to sound too eager.

Bryndis frowned. 'You won't be too long, will you? Or we'll have to leave without you.'

'No, I promise. I don't want to get stuck here!' Tia waved and left the kitchen.

She went straight to where her friends had told her Skadi's forbidden tower was. To her surprise

30

there weren't any guards at the bottom of the stairs. She quickly crept up the stone steps. It was pitch black but she didn't dare spark a flame for fear of alerting the guards she was sure were at the top of the stairs. She put one hand on either side of the cold stone walls and felt her way upwards. The steps were broken and crumbling and she stumbled twice. *I suppose, as Skadi can use the sapphire to transport herself, she doesn't need to use stairs,* Tia thought. *That's why she hasn't bothered to mend them.*

At last the spiral stairs came to an end and opened into a small circular hall dimly lit with an ethereal blue glow. On either side was an archway. One had a door with a lock, the other was doorless and the ghostly blue light was coming from inside the room. Tia decided the locked door probably led to Skadi's apartments while the doorless room surely contained the sapphire. Only a jewel with strong magic could give off such a beautiful light.

There was still no sign of guards. Tia crept round the walls up to the open archway and looked cautiously inside.

Resting on a white marble block in the middle of the room was a silver bracelet set with a huge, glowing sapphire. Stationed around the room stood six massive guards. They were carved out of marble in the form of huge trolls, snarling and baring broken fangs. Each gripped a club in fists tipped with talons.

Skadi had cast such strong magic on them that the air crackled with it. Tia was sure that the minute the trolls knew she was there they'd turn on her. *I can't fight them!* she thought. But there had to be a way to trick them; trolls were stupid creatures and there was no reason to suppose that marble ones were any cleverer.

She stared hard at the trolls and began to see glimmering silver threads of magic beaming from their eyes. The magical rays wove a criss-cross web around the room. She guessed that if anyone touched one of the magical beams it would set off an alarm to make the trolls attack and bring Skadi rushing from her rooms.

Tia frowned. There had to be a way through. But no matter how hard she tried she couldn't see one. The only way to reach the jewel would be to climb over, and wriggle under, the beams.

She took a tentative step forward then thought, *There isn't enough time to try now – I've been here long enough already.*

She drew back, tiptoed through the hall and went back down the steps. As she entered the corridors

she realised with a shock that faint daylight was filtering through the windows. She ran as fast as she could for the kitchen.

But she was too late. Her friends had gone.

She could hear stirrings in the castle as servants began getting ready for the new day. She sprinted to the watergate. It was shut and there was no sign of the boat.

Tia gripped the iron bars and the gate opened. Ingvar had left it unlocked.

That was one problem solved, but now she had to swim the moat. Well, it was her own fault she'd lost track of time; she'd have to make the best of it.

She took off her gold chain with its locket and the emerald ring and put them safely in her coat pocket before she took it off. Then she kicked off her boots and wrapped them in her coat. Holding the bundle above her head she slid into the smelly water. She swam across one-handed, keeping her coat clear of the water. It took her much longer than if she had been swimming freely and she was freezing when she got to the other side. She clambered onto the bank and dressed as quickly as she could.

By the time Tia had dragged on her boots and coat and refastened her chain with fumbling, icy hands, the sun had risen. She made sure the way was clear before she made a dash from the trees, ran through the backstreets and skidded down the deserted alley. She rapped gently on the trapdoor. 'It's me, Tia,' she said softly. 'Let me in!'

She heard a bolt being drawn back and looked round quickly to check that no-one was turning onto the street. Perched on a window ledge was a jackdaw. Before she could decide if it was Loki, the trapdoor opened and Ingvar grabbed her, pulled her into the cellar and re-bolted the trapdoor.

Sindri rushed up and flung his arms round her. 'I thought you'd been taken!'

'I'm sorry,' Tia said hugging him tightly.

'So you should be.' Bryndis glared at her. 'He was worried about you.'

'Thanks for leaving the watergate unlocked,' Tia said to Ingvar.

'Don't expect me to do it again.' He glared even more fiercely than his sister.

'You're all wet and you smell!' Sindri said.

Tia wrinkled her nose. She did smell. 'I had to swim the moat.'

'You can borrow some of my clothes for today. We'll wash yours at the castle tonight,' Bryndis said.

'Thank you.' Tia smiled but Bryndis simply handed over the clothes and went with Sindri to lie down with her face to the wall. Ingvar did the same. Tia was in disgrace.

She quickly changed and lay in her sleeping place. She shivered; even with her coat on top of the blankets she was still chilled from the moat. She hoped she'd warm up quickly. She hoped even more that Bryndis and Ingvar would forgive her soon.

After they'd finished their tasks that night and sat at the castle fireside where Tia's newly washed clothes steamed in the heat, Sindri held up his fist. 'Look what I found.' He waved three glossy feathers, two black and one grey.

'They're pretty,' Tia said. 'Where did you find them?'

'On the ground, by the trapdoor.' Sindri stuck the feathers in his hair and ran round the kitchen pretending he could fly.

Ingvar and Bryndis laughed and joined in but Tia stayed by the fire, thinking.

The feathers were from a jackdaw. Loki must have left them as a sign he knew where she was.

She could leave a message in return and he'd take it to Finn.

The next day, while the others were sleeping, she took her silver-tipped pen and green book out of her bag and wrote:

Finn – I am well. I have discovered where the next object is. I will take it soon. T.

She tore the page out, rolled it up and tied it with a piece of thread pulled from her shirt. That night, when they went through the trapdoor, Tia dropped the message. When they returned, the paper had gone.

Chapter Five

The Great Statue

Tia worked very hard during the next few days. She scrubbed and sewed in the castle kitchens at night and sat at the table with Sindri, helping him learn his runes, when the work was done. Back in the cellar she told him stories of Prince Kaspar and the Skrimsli Bear before he went to sleep. Very often she saw Bryndis and Ingvar listening too. She pretended not to notice and concentrated on telling the tales as skilfully as she could. She always ended with a soft sweet lullaby that sent Sindri off to sleep.

'Where did you learn that song?' Bryndis asked one morning.

'I don't know,' Tia said. To her surprise she realised it was true. It wasn't a Trader song or a DragonSong so where had she heard it? For a fleeting moment she thought she remembered a warm embrace and a woman singing sweetly, then the memory was gone. 'I've just always known it.'

When Tia settled down later and fell asleep, the song was echoing in her mind.

A sound of cheering and the blare of a trumpet woke Tia. A second blast of sound had Bryndis, Ingvar and Sindri shooting up from their blankets.

'What was that?' Sindri said.

'Let's find out.' Ingvar unbolted the trapdoor and raised it cautiously. Tia joined him and they looked down the street to the square. 'It's a procession,' Tia said. 'Where are they going? Why are they so excited?'

'No idea. Wait here, I'll go and see.' Ingvar climbed up into the deserted street. He walked a little way, paused in a doorway and watched the excited crowd.

Tia was annoyed. If Ingvar could go out in the daytime then why couldn't she? She scrambled into the street, ignoring Bryndis's fierce, 'Stop!', and joined Ingvar in the doorway.

'What's going on?' she asked.

Ingvar glared at her. 'You should be in the cellar.'

'I wanted to see.'

More and more people were lining the square. The excitement built. A trumpet sounded again.

'There it is!' A man pointed to the open gates. The whole crowd started cheering and clapping as a team of eight horses hauled a waggon into the square. It stopped and Tia gasped. In the waggon, secured by ropes, was an enormous marble statue glistening white in the sunshine.

'It's Skadi.' Tia turned and saw Bryndis staring open-mouthed in astonishment at the statue. Sindri was hopping up and down in excitement beside her.

'Let me see!'

'Hush, in a minute,' Bryndis said.

Tia turned back to the scene in front of her. So this was Skadi, feared High Witch of Iserborg – and her fourth aunt. The sculpture was magnificent: dignified and with a beautiful face, though Tia thought the lips were twisted in a cruel smile.

A herald rode up to the waggon. He blew a fanfare on his trumpet and the crowd stopped shouting and listened.

'All you subjects of the mighty High Witch, the Lady Skadi, are ordered to gather before her at the gates of the castle,' he announced.He blew his

trumpet again and led the waggon towards the castle. The crowd surged after it, leaping and cheering.

'I wonder what Skadi wants now,' Ingvar said.

Tia wondered that too.

'It's too dangerous to follow,' Bryndis said. 'We have to get back to the cellar.' She reached out her hand to her little brother. He wasn't there.

'Where's Sindri?' Bryndis looked round wildly.

Tia pointed at the end of the procession. 'There he is!'

Sindri was skipping into the crowd hurrying to the castle.

'You should've held onto his hand, Bryndis,' Ingvar said.

'And you shouldn't have left the cellar in the first place,' his sister blazed back.

Tia knew they were angry because they were scared, but arguing wasn't going to do any good. 'I'll go and get him,' she said.

'We'll all go. It'll give us a better chance of finding him,' Ingvar said firmly.

Leaving a safe gap between themselves and the end of the crowd, the three children followed until the waggon lumbered to a stop in front of the castle. They hid behind a cart and watched as the men driving the team of horses climbed into the waggon and cut the ropes keeping the statue from toppling over. The throng fell silent. It waited anxiously. Tia wondered what for.

Then a gasp rippled through the gathering. Skadi had appeared out of nowhere to stand in front of the waggon. She had her hand on the arm of a man who'd appeared with her.

Tia gasped too, not just at the sight of her beautiful aunt with a streak of white zigzagging through her dark hair like a bolt of lightning, but also at the man.

He was shorter than Skadi, and very strong-looking. And he resembled the portrait of Tia's father that she carried in her locket: his eyes were as dark, his hair as black and curly and he had the same curving nose.

The crowd began to cheer and call out, 'Long live the Lady Skadi!'

The witch held up her hand and the gathering instantly stopped shouting. 'My people, as you can see, Master Zeno has completed his tribute to me.' She gestured at the statue and then at the man beside her. He bowed and helped Skadi onto the waggon. She put her hand on the statue.

'He has brought this to me but cannot take it to the place where all can see and admire it.' She pointed to an alcove cut into the stone above the castle gates. Before Tia could even blink, the statue was inside the alcove with Skadi standing on the ledge next to it. In the time it took Tia to draw breath in amazement, the witch was back beside Zeno.

She smiled in the cruel way the statue did. 'The Master Sculptor will accompany me to dinner where he will be my guest of honour.' The witch laid her hand on Zeno's arm again and they vanished.

The crowd let out a final gasp, this time of relief. Skadi wasn't coming back, at least for now. Little groups formed, chatting and laughing or talking solemnly, shaking their heads and pointing up at the statue.

Tia leaned against a cart. No wonder everyone in Iserborg was jumpy and tense! Although she'd known Skadi used the sapphire to transport herself from place to place, she hadn't known the witch could carry people – and statues – with her. That was what people meant when they said Skadi 'took' men for the quarries or women and children for servants. Tia wondered what had happened to her friends' mother. Where had Skadi 'taken' her?

Bryndis elbowed Tia. 'There's Sindri,' she whispered. The little boy was near the front of the crowd, gaping at the statue, entranced. 'You stay here,' Bryndis ordered. 'We'll get him.' She and Ingvar moved off.

'Where've you been?' a voice said close to Tia's ear. She nearly jumped out of her skin.

'Loki!' The jackdaw was perched on the cart. Tia quickly explained where and why she hid in the daytime and what she'd discovered about Skadi and the sapphire. 'I'm going to get into that room as soon as I can and steal it.'

She pulled a fat wad of paper out of her pocket.

'I've written it all down for you to take to Finn. It's quite a big message, I'll need to tie it on.'

With a shake of his head, Loki held out a leg and Tia fastened the package on with twine she'd found in the castle. 'There, it's done. Thank you, Loki.' Tia stroked the bird's grey head.

'I'll be back to keep an eye on you,' he said. 'At least you haven't been captured again – yet.' He took off and was soon out of sight.

Tia sighed. She missed him, and she missed her DragonBrother even more.

Chapter Six

Master Zeno

When Tia and the children were safely back in the cellar Ingvar insisted they make rules. 'It's the best way to stay safe,' he said.

Tia agreed, though she knew she wouldn't be able to keep all the rules, not if she was going to steal the sapphire.

'We need to be responsible for each other,' Ingvar said. 'And us older ones have to look out for Sindri especially.'

'No-one must be late leaving the castle.' Bryndis glared at Tia. 'If they get left behind, Skadi might capture them and make them tell where the others are.'

Ingvar nodded in agreement. Tia did too, but her face went hot with embarrassment. Bryndis made it sound as though Tia had been late deliberately. But even if she had been captured by the High Witch she'd never have told Skadi about Bryndis and her brothers.

'And Sindri,' Ingvar spoke sternly to the little boy, 'you must promise not to wander off. Always tell one of us where you want to go and ask permission.'

Sindri nodded. 'And you mustn't wander off either,' he said earnestly to Tia.

'All right,' she agreed, feeling terrible because she didn't mean what she was saying.

They spat on their palms and linked hands to seal the promise.

Sindri yawned. It made Bryndis laugh. 'Let's get some sleep before we go to work tonight.'

Tia wanted to sleep but she tossed and turned, trying to think of a way to steal the sapphire without breaking her promise to her friends. She couldn't think of a thing and it was a long time before she dropped off to sleep.

That night the children were in for a shock. When they reached the castle kitchen they were just in time to see a servant woman, carrying a tray, bustling out of the door.

'What's she doing?' Bryndis asked quietly as the woman turned a corner at the end of the corridor.

'No idea,' Ingvar said. 'Let's check there's no-one else in the kitchen.' It was empty.

Tia picked up a note lying on the kitchen table and read it out:

Noble Elves,

Master Zeno, the sculptor, is carving a marble fireplace in the great hall for the lady Skadi. He often works late and we have to take him food and drink.

We will knock on the kitchen door and wait a while before we enter.

We do not wish to offend you. Please do not leave the castle.

'That explains it,' Ingvar said. 'It shouldn't interfere with our work if we're careful. Let's find a place where we can hide quickly when we hear the knock.'

They decided on a large cupboard where the brooms were kept. 'She won't go in here if she's just serving food,' Bryndis said.

'Especially if we sweep the floor clean first!' Tia grinned.

The four children worked silently at their tasks in case the servant woman came back, heard them chatting, and realised they weren't elves at all, only lost children.

Sure enough, after a while, there was a tap on the door and a voice said politely, 'O elves, I must enter.'

The children squashed into the cupboard and closed the door. There were little ornamental holes carved in the wood and they were able to spy through them.

'I am entering now,' the voice said and the servant woman came in. She glanced around, the firelight reflecting on her anxious face. Bryndis and Ingvar drew a quick breath of surprise.

They've recognised her, Tia thought. *I wonder who she is?*

The woman put her tray on the table, hurried to the door, turned and curtseyed. 'Thank you, elves. I shall leave you in peace till tomorrow.' She went out and the children tumbled from the cupboard.

'Who was she?' Tia asked.

The older brother and sister exchanged a glance. 'It was our Aunt Tinna,' Ingvar said, 'our mother's sister.'

'She looked nice,' Tia said. Tinna had a round, friendly face and if she hadn't been worried Tia was sure she'd have been smiling. 'Couldn't she care for you?'

Ingvar shrugged. 'I think she wanted to after Mother was taken – she was always very kind – but it would've put her in danger so we didn't ask.'

She won't be in danger after I take the sapphire, Tia thought. She was relieved to know there'd be someone to care for her friends once she'd stolen the sapphire and left Iserborg. But first she wanted to know more about Zeno, the Master Sculptor. He looked so like her father, he had to be from over the Southern Sea. He might even know Elio, or at least have heard of him.

She paused in her work and patted the locket under her shirt where she kept her father's picture. It might be risky but if she spoke to Master Zeno alone, if she was ready to run at the first sign of danger, then surely it was worth taking a chance to find out about her father?

She scrubbed away at a muddy boot, more determined than ever to speak to Master Zeno as soon as she could.

Her chance came a few days later. They were in the cellar, waiting for night to fall, and Sindri was drawing a wolf. He'd used Tia's silverpoint pen and a sheet from her book.

'That's very good,' Ingvar said. 'You'll be an artist one day.'

Sindri beamed. 'I can be like Master Zeno and make carvings. Can we go and see his new ones in the Great Hall?'

His brother and sister exchanged a glance.

Please say yes! Tia thought.

'I don't see why not,' Bryndis said. 'Aunt Tinna always brings back Master Zeno's tray at the same time. We could wait until she's done that and then go and look at the carvings.'

Ingvar agreed. Tia heaved a sigh of relief and set her plan in action.

She'd decided to leave the emerald behind. No matter how kind Master Zeno might be, he was bound to be suspicious of a girl who owned a huge jewel set in a gold ring. She'd already prised up a stone in the floor under her bedding and scooped out some soil. Now she took the ring off her chain, wrapped it in a piece of rag, dropped it in the hollow and replaced the stone.

Hurriedly she tidied her blankets and re-fastened her chain.

Ingvar was unbolting the trapdoor. 'Hurry up, snail!' he said to Tia.

'I'm coming.'

Tia followed the others through Iserborg town and into the castle. Her heart beat fast. Tonight, at long last, she might hear news of her father.

Chapter Seven

Trapped

The children peeped out from behind one of the columns running down the two long sides of the Great Hall. At the far end sat Master Zeno, looking intently at the marble fireplace.

'I can't see the carvings properly, can we get any closer?' Sindri whispered.

Ingvar nodded. 'We can dodge behind these pillars if we're very careful.'

The four children went silently from column to column until they were as close as they dared go. Master Zeno kept looking from a drawing he held in his hand to an unfinished sculpture of a strange creature hanging upside down from the top of the fireplace. It had a body like a giant mouse with wings sprouting from its back. Its open mouth was filled with fangs and each wing ended in a bony finger tipped with a claw.

Sindri's mouth formed an 'O' of astonishment. His eyes grew even rounder as he stared at the other strange and sinister marble animals creeping over the fireplace. Tia wondered why Master Zeno had created such ugly creatures. It must be because that was what Skadi had ordered him to do.

It was cold in the hall and Sindri began to shiver. Bryndis tapped his shoulder and pointed back up the long corridor. The sister and brothers tiptoed away but Tia stayed where she was. Halfway up, Bryndis turned, a puzzled look on her face. She flapped her hand urgently at Tia to signal she had to hurry and catch up.

Tia mouthed, *Sorry*, and stepped out into the hall. She went up to the sculptor. 'Master Zeno?'

He turned and rocked back on his stool in surprise. He swiftly looked Tia over, his eyebrows bunching darkly above the bridge of his curved nose. Tia thought he might shout at her for disturbing him, and got ready to run. But a warm friendly smile spread over his face. 'Why, it's a child. What can I do for you, my dear?'

Tia smiled back. 'I'd like to ask you a question.'
'Of course.'
'Are you from over the Southern Sea, Master?'
'Yes, I am.'

Tia took out her locket and opened it. 'This is a picture of my father, Elio. He's from the same place as you and I wondered if you'd heard of him.'

The sculptor rose from his stool and reached out. But instead of taking the locket in his hand as Tia expected, he seized her arm and yelled, 'Guards! Guards!'

Tia struggled but the man's grip was hard. The more she wriggled and kicked the tighter he held her.

Two guards rushed in. 'This is the thief girl, Nadya, wanted by the Lady Skadi – summon her immediately!' Zeno shouted.

One of the guards ran out in the direction of Skadi's tower and the second seized Tia's other arm. She couldn't believe what had happened. The Master Sculptor had looked so kind with his smiling face. She had put her friends in danger for no reason – and got herself captured.

Skadi swept into the hall escorted by several more guards. Her cloak flew out behind her and her hair streamed down her back, making the white streak look more like a bolt of lightning than ever. The sapphire glittered from the bracelet on her arm.

'So, this is our little jewel thief,' Skadi said, a note of triumph in her voice.

Tia glared at the sculptor as he pushed her forward and bowed extravagantly to the High Witch.

'Indeed it is, my lady. And I claim my reward of five hundred silver marks.'

That was all he wanted! He'd tricked Tia for money. Why had she allowed her eagerness to find out about her father blind her to danger?

Skadi waved him away. 'I shall question the girl first and then we shall see.'

'But, Lady...'

Skadi swung round and snapped, 'I said, we shall see.'

'Of course, Lady.' The sculptor bowed again and hurriedly backed away.

If Tia hadn't been scared, she'd have laughed. Zeno's expression was a mixture of fury, frustration and resentment. All trace of the friendly smile was gone. He left, darting evil glances at Tia.

Skadi ordered the guard to let go of Tia and all the soldiers withdrew to the edges of the hall. Then she touched Tia's shoulder. For a moment she wondered if the witch was going to 'take' her but she simply drew Tia inside her cloak and smiled down encouragingly. It didn't fool Tia for a second.

'I think you should give me the jewels, Nadya – the emerald, the opal and the topaz.'

'I'm not Nadya and I haven't got any jewels, Lady.'

'Shall we see? Empty your pockets.'

Skadi kept her hand tightly on Tia's shoulder as she turned her pockets inside out. There was nothing in them.

'Hmm.' Skadi pointed to the locket Tia clutched in her hand. 'What's that?'

Tia reluctantly showed her. 'This is a picture of my father.' Tia's mouth went dry. Elio was married to Skadi's youngest sister – what if she recognized his portrait? 'Papa went missing and I've been searching all Tulay for him,' Tia gabbled. 'I've looked in Drangur, Kulafoss and Stoplar – that's probably why I got confused with this thief. I reached Iserborg a few days ago and saw Master Zeno with your beautiful statue.'

Tia snapped the locket shut and rushed on with her explanation of why she'd spoken to the sculptor, hoping that Skadi would lose interest in the locket if she chattered enough.

'Enough!' Skadi held up her hand. 'I don't believe this story of a lost father.' To Tia's relief she waved away the locket. 'You are Nadya the jewel thief, and you will tell me where they are.'

'I'm not so I can't!' Tia twisted free and shot away from the witch. She swerved around a guard and ran up the hall. Suddenly Skadi appeared in front of her. Tia skidded to a halt, her heart jumping into her throat. She backed away and bumped into a column. Skadi sneered. Tia swung round the column only to find herself face to face with the witch again. Skadi threw back her head and laughed. Tia ran down the hall and up the stairs with the witch's laughter echoing at her back. And then the mocking laughter was in front of her as Skadi appeared out of nowhere.

Though it was hopeless, Tia still ran. She sidestepped and sprinted this way and that but Skadi was always ahead of her, always laughing. When Tia had no breath left for running, she knew she had lost. Her legs folded and she slumped at the witch's feet.

Skadi reached down and touched Tia's arm. Instantly they were in the middle of a field of geysers, gushing out steam and squirting boiling water high in the air.

Chapter Eight

Geysers
and volcanoes

Skadi had taken Tia to the edge of an isolated plain. They stood on top of a high boulder in the middle of a tumble of rocks sloping down towards the geysers. All around them the geysers steamed, spraying out a vile smell, or threw spouts of boiling white water with a tremendous whooshing into the night sky.

Tia was dizzy and sick. Being 'taken' felt horrible. To make things worse, the ground suddenly shook and Tia almost lost her footing. An eerie red glow lit up the darkness.

Skadi laughed. 'This is the edge of my land of Iserborg and behind you lies Askarlend and its volcanoes. No-one, not even my sister, Hyldi, who rules there, knows when they will erupt.' The witch sounded amused that her sister lived in constant danger. She spun Tia around. 'And there is her castle, the one you will never reach now that you are in my power.'

Tia couldn't help gasping in amazement. Hyldi's castle rose up on the other side of the empty land lying between Iserborg and Askarlend, and it was enormous. But what astonished Tia more than its size were the lights that covered it, flashing in every colour imaginable.

'You'll have plenty of time to stare at my sister's ugly castle.' Skadi shuddered with distaste, though Tia thought her castle was just as horrible as Hyldi's. 'And don't imagine you can escape or you'll end up caught by the geysers like those poor fools.' Skadi sneered down at moonlit white bones scattered on the ground.

Tia bit her lip to stop herself from crying out. She wasn't going to show fear in front of her cruel aunt.

'I'll be back in two days,' Skadi said. 'By then I'm sure you'll have remembered where you've hidden the three jewels.'

'I told you, I don't know...' Tia protested but found herself talking to thin air. Skadi had transported herself back to Iserborg.

Tia passed the rest of the night on top of the rock. She sat hugging her knees, her chin propped on top of them and tried to think of a way around her problem. Finn and Loki couldn't help; they didn't know she'd been taken. Nor did it help that she had witch powers, except for being able to make fire to keep warm.

Gloomily Tia waited for the sun to rise and watched the geysers jetting water into the moonlight. Mesmerised by their rhythmical dance, she nodded off to sleep. With a start she woke from her doze. She mustn't fall asleep again and risk falling down the boulder into a geyser.

She shook her head. She must have slept for quite a while as the sun was lighting up the horizon. It was all the geysers' fault, she thought, with their hypnotic pulse lulling her to sleep. She glared at the nearest one as though it was doing it on purpose: whoosh-spout, whoosh-spout, pause, pause, whoosh-spout! It was enough to make anyone drift off.

As Tia scowled, a narrow gap opened between the geysers just in front of her and also the ones behind them. They'd spouted and paused together. Tia jumped to her feet. She watched carefully and saw that the geysers all gushed and stopped in a sequence. And sometimes they cleared, just for a second, one after the other. Perhaps there was a way through after all.

Tia counted carefully over and over again. Eventually she worked out the pattern. If she was right she would be able to run through the geysers as they paused one after the other. She counted a few more times. Yes, she could do it – she was sure!

She waited for the beginning of the sequence and, just as it was about to start, ran down the sloping boulder and into the geysers as the first row sank into the hot ground.

She stumbled as the unexpectedly crusty surface cracked under her boots. Frantically she scrabbled upright and ran as the geyser behind whooshed up again. She pelted forward, always reaching the geysers in front of her as they sank into their pools of glopping mud, and the ones behind shot upwards. It was hard to breathe in the stifling air smelling like a thousand bad eggs, but she didn't pause for a second.

And then she was breathing cool, fresh air and her feet were running on grass.

She carried on sprinting until she was sure it was safe to turn and look back.

Yes! She'd made it! She'd escaped! That would show Skadi. Tia yelled in triumph and turned cartwheels till she ran out of energy and flopped onto the grass.

Now all she had to do was find her way back to Iserborg town and steal the sapphire.

Tia used the position of the sun to guide her back to Iserborg. The way was over gently sloping hills dotted with thickets of trees and though the walk was long it wasn't difficult. She kept up a steady pace all day and at sunset she settled by a stream running through a small wood. After she'd drunk the cool, clear water she made a fire to curl up next to. She ignored her hunger pangs. *It's better to be hungry and warm than fed and cold*, she thought, and quickly fell asleep.

As soon as she woke the next morning she started off again. She arrived at Iserborg, hungry and footsore, that evening. She joined a bunch of quarrymen hurrying down the avenue of beasts towards the town. The raggle-taggle group surged through the gates as the guards were drawing them closed. No-one took any notice of Tia as she rushed through with the latecomers. Nor did they give her a second glance as she sauntered across the square and into the side road.

She crouched in shadows near the trapdoor, waiting till it was fully dark. While she waited she wondered what her friends would think when they saw her. She expected they'd be angry with her for putting them in even greater danger than before. Maybe they wouldn't want to help her any more?

The trapdoor opened and the three children climbed into the street. Tia walked out into the moonlight. 'Don't be afraid,' she said softly. 'It's me, Tia.'

The three children stood stock still and stared as if she were a ghost.

'But you were taken,' Ingvar said.

Tia went closer. 'I escaped. I've been walking for two days without any food. I'm so hungry.'

They still stood frozen to the spot.

'I didn't mean to cause trouble,' Tia said. 'I only spoke to Master Zeno because...'

'You wanted to ask him about your father,' Bryndis

said. 'I came back for you and heard everything. When he called for the guards I ran away.'

To Tia's astonishment, Bryndis hugged her. 'I would do the same to find my mother.'

'Me too,' Ingvar said gruffly. 'Though I'd trust the rest of you enough to tell you what I was going to do.'

Sindri reached shyly for Tia's hand as though he was trying to decide if she was real or not.

'We've got some food in the cellar,' Bryndis said. 'Come and have that and then sleep while we work. You can tell us all about what happened when we come back in the morning.'

'And we'll bring more food,' Ingvar promised.

Tia wearily climbed into the cellar. She ate the pastries the children gave her then lay down. Once she was settled, her friends left for the castle. Tia was so tired she only just managed to turn down the oil lamp before she fell fast asleep.

Chapter Nine

Battle with the trolls

Tia was in a muddle. Ingvar had said they ought to trust each other, and she did trust him, and Bryndis. She even trusted little Sindri though he was too young to be told everything. Of course, she had trusted Zeno, and see where that had got her. But her friends had looked after her and shared their hiding place with her.

All the same, Tia knew she couldn't tell them about her life with the dragons or her mission to recover their jewels. And she certainly couldn't reveal the fact that she had witch powers. No, she had to accept that she couldn't share her secrets with anyone.

Once her mind was made up, Tia felt better and when the children returned from the castle with lots more food, she forgot her problems as she ate.

When she'd finished her friends listened eagerly as she told them about being 'taken' by Skadi.

'What did it feel like?' Sindri asked.

'Horrible! It makes you go wobbly and sick.'

'Do you think our mother might've been taken to the same place?' Bryndis wanted to know.

Tia shook her head. 'There was no sign,' she said. She wasn't going to mention the bones.

'Skadi does take people to faraway places like farms and mills,' Ingvar said. 'She makes them work for her and locks them up at night. Maybe Mother will come back one day, like you have.'

Tia knew that when she'd stolen the sapphire her friends would be free to talk to their Aunt Tinna and she could help them look for their mother. 'If Skadi didn't have the sapphire, the people in Iserborg could take the town back and keep her in the castle where she can't do any harm. They've done it to the High Witches in Drangur, Kulafoss and Stoplar.'

'How do you know that?' Bryndis asked. 'Is it because you really are the jewel thief?'

Tia held out her hands, palms up. 'Have you seen me with any jewels?'

The three children shook their heads.

'I'm sure if I had the topaz and the opal you'd see me using them.' She was glad Finn had persuaded her to let him look after those gems. She had used them and found it difficult to stop. She didn't mention the emerald, which she was sitting on at that moment.

'I suppose that's true,' Ingvar admitted.

'I heard about what happened to the witches when I was travelling. The jewels always seemed to be stolen when I was there.' That was true.

Bryndis laughed. 'As you're here now, do you think the sapphire will be stolen too?'

Tia grinned. 'I expect so.'

'Then you can move on to look for your father. Where will you try next?' Ingvar asked.

'Askarlend – then Holmurholt.' Tia tried not to think about Holmurholt. It was where her mother Ondine, youngest of the six High Witches, lived.

Sindri flung his arms round Tia. 'But you're going to stay with us a bit longer, aren't you?'

Tia hugged him back. 'Oh, at least till tomorrow!'

There were no more questions then. The children seemed happy with Tia's answers, and they settled down to sleep.

Tia lay down too, but when the others were asleep she quietly lifted her blankets, prised up the loose stone, took out the emerald ring and threaded it back on her chain.

She'd slept so long already that she was wide awake, so she concentrated on thinking about how to steal the sapphire. She planned to do it that night. She was sure she could get through the trolls' magic beams without raising the alarm. Then, before Skadi was awake, she'd leave by the watergate with her friends, as usual. She'd wait for the guards to open the town gates at dawn, follow the quarrymen down the Avenue of Beasts and wait for Loki to find her. When he did she'd ask him to fly the jewel, and a message, to Finn.

She smiled at the thought of seeing her DragonBrother again. He might even disguise himself to fool the spell and come to pick her up in his scaly arms. That would save her a walk!

She turned over and dozed off, dreaming she was back in the Drakelow Mountains, curled up against her beloved DragonMother in her warm familiar cavern.

'Time to go!' Ingvar unlocked the trapdoor and they climbed into the street. He and Sindri walked ahead while Tia and Bryndis followed.

'You've brought your bag with you tonight – are you leaving?' Bryndis asked softly.

'Yes,' Tia said. 'I didn't find my parents and it's time to move on. Besides, I don't want Skadi to know I escaped.' All those facts were true. 'I'll help you with the tasks tonight and leave in the morning.'

'Will we see you again?'

'I hope so.'

'We'll miss you.'

'I'll miss you too.' Tia had grown to like her friends very much. Not as much as Finn but he was her DragonBrother and she loved him.

At the castle they did their jobs as usual, hid from Tinna, and played games after she'd gone. While her friends were absorbed in throwing dice Tia quietly left the kitchen and made her way to the High Witch's tower rooms. She went up the dark stairway, darted through the blue-lit hall and sneaked a look into the troll room. Nothing had changed.

Tia set her bag by the archway and concentrated on the rays streaming from the trolls' eyes. She could take her time but she had to be sure she didn't touch one of the beams of magic and set off an alarm.

She took a deep breath, made sure her jacket wasn't flapping loose and stepped over the first beam. The trolls didn't move. She was safe!

Bit by bit she worked her way over and under the rays of magic until she reached the marble block with the silver bracelet resting on the top. The sapphire was held in a setting running round the jewel's edge like a belt. That meant one side always lay on the wearer's skin while the other side was on show.

And what a show it was! The sapphire glowed like the purest blue sky on a summer's day. Tia wanted to stare into its depths for ever.

She reached out and carefully picked up the bracelet. The trolls didn't move. Tia slid the bracelet onto her wrist, feeling the sapphire against her skin, its power seeping into her. She lifted her arm and the jewel glowed at her.

Tia's mind swam, filled with the beauty and power of the blue stone. Why didn't she just transport herself straight to Askarlend? She could do it with no problem at all...

No! She'd promised Finn she'd never use the jewels. She shook her head, stumbled backwards as her mind cleared, and trod on one of the gossamer rays of magic.

The beams turned red, piercing the sapphire's heavenly blue light with a lurid crimson. It lit up the trolls' faces, staining their broken fangs as they ground their jaws. With a ghastly grating noise they raised their clubs and swivelled towards Tia, their red eyes pulsing.

Tia pelted for the archway. Two trolls reached it before her. They crammed into the space at the same time and trapped themselves. Before they could wrench their bodies free, or the other trolls could reach her, Tia snatched up her bag and squeezed between their stone legs into the hall.

'You!' Skadi stood in the doorway to her rooms, staring in furious shock.

'Yes, me!' Tia sprang forward towards the stairs but a marble fist caught her bag. Her jacket sleeve slid up her arm, showing the bracelet.

'My sapphire!' Skadi screamed.

In panic Tia pushed at the troll's hand gripping her bag. Why hadn't she just transported herself to Askarlend when she had the chance? An image of Hyldi's castle flashed through her mind –

And then she was there. The sprawling, ungainly building loomed above her, lights flashing and music ringing from every window and door. Tia had transported herself there without meaning to. And she'd brought the troll with her!

'Ugh?' He let go of Tia and stared round in bewilderment before the last of Skadi's magic drained out of him and he turned to nothing more than a statue again.

Tia hurriedly pulled down her sleeve to hide the glowing sapphire and walked away with her head down. While people were excitedly gathering round the marble troll who'd suddenly appeared in their midst, they weren't bothering with her.

When she reached a quiet little square with a fountain splashing in the middle, she slid off the bracelet and put it in her pocket. She sat on the wall surrounding the fountain and thought about Skadi. The commotion she'd made would alert everyone in the castle and they'd soon realise she couldn't 'take' people any more or switch from place to place in the blink of an eye. Surely they'd overpower her and spread the good news among the townsfolk? Then, when Loki patrolled Iserborg he'd see cheerful people, realize what had happened and report to Finn.

Tia brightened at the thought – then frowned. It might still take her friends some time to work out that she was already in Askarlend. Perhaps she ought to use the sapphire and return to them now? It was easy; she hadn't felt sick or dizzy when she'd transported herself.

Before she knew what she was doing the bracelet was in her hand and she was gazing into the sapphire's entrancing blue glow.

She closed her eyes. No – the jewels were too powerful for her to control; that was why she'd promised her DragonBrother never to use them. She shoved the bracelet back in her pocket. She had to wait till Finn and Loki came looking for her.

Until then she needed a safe place to stay and a way to earn her food.

She pulled her jacket tightly round herself, slung her bag on her back, and set off to explore this flashing, noisy town she'd arrived in by mistake.

Can Tia and her friends meet the challenge of
the fifth adventure? Find out in

The Ruby Quest

published by Bloomsbury
March 2014